This book belongs to:

....

For Anita, with thanks – C.F.

HODDER CHILDREN'S BOOKS

First published in Great Britain in 2020 by Hodder and Stoughton

Text and illustrations © Charles Fuge, 2020 • The moral rights of the author/illustrator have been asserted.

All rights reserved • A CIP catalogue record for this book is available from the British Library.

HB ISBN: 978 1 444 94812 7 • PB ISBN: 978 1 444 94813 4

1 3 5 7 9 10 8 6 4 2 • Printed and bound in China.

Hodder Children's Books, an imprint of Hachette Children's Group, part of Hodder and Stoughton

Carmelite House, 50 Victoria Embankment, London, EC4Y 0DZ • An Hachette UK Company

www.hachette.co.uk • www.hachettechildrens.co.uk

Together

Charles Fuge

As you look at the world
from the safety of home,
though the sky is so vast,
you won't feel alone.

Though the land seems to go
on **for ever** and **ever**,

you'll never be lonely. . .

because we're together.

Together we **wander**
and **wonder** at things . . .

in the **warmth** of the sun,
with the **joy** that it brings.

And when we're together, we don't mind the cold.

We'll always have each other's warm hand to hold!

We often imagine faraway lands,
with parrots and palm trees and
warm golden sands.

But then we agree that we

don't need that stuff...

just being together is
more than enough!

Sometimes at night, we gaze at the stars
and we talk about Pluto and Venus and Mars.
You learn new things fast, because you're SO clever . . .

and learning's such fun,

when we are together!

Together we stand,

together we ... fall.

Together we travel, one big and one small.

Together we laugh and we sing and we

play . . .

enjoying togetherness every day!

And when you feel worried, and you ask me whether I might ever leave you, I always say, "NEVER!"

"Together!" you say, as we cuddle up tight.

"For ever," I whisper, and kiss you goodnight.